MW00748848

Santa
REX

by
Molly Idle

VIKING

EXPECTING company for Christmas?

The more the merrier!

With everyone helping, all your holiday preparations will be done in no time.

Deck the halls with boughs of holly,

paper chains,

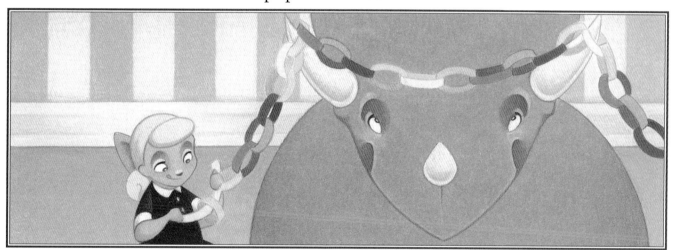

strings of popcorn,

and cut-out window snowflakes.

Everyone loves to help bake Christmas cookies.

So delicious, they're sure to disappear quickly.

Be sure to save a few for Santa . . .

. . . when he comes down the chimney to fill your stockings.

But if you don't have a fireplace, you can hang them anywhere you like. Santa will know what to do.

When it's time to trim the tree,

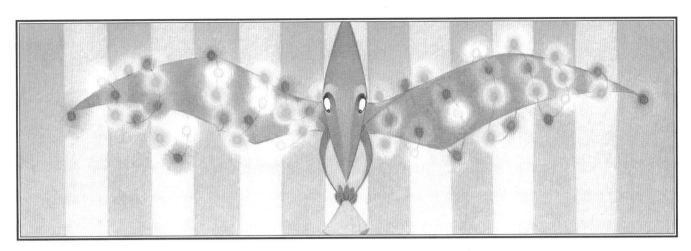

put on the lights first,

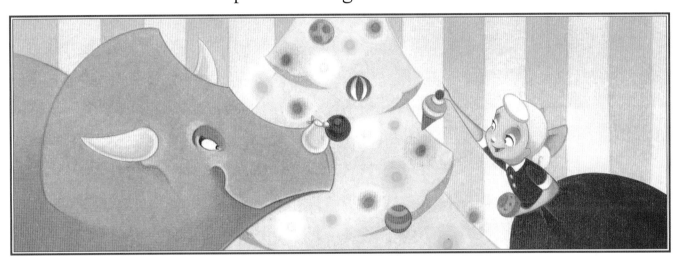

then the ornaments,

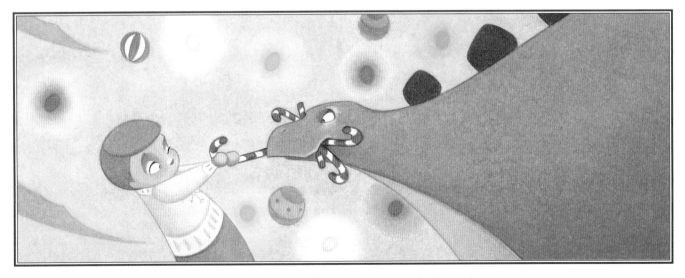

then the candy canes and tinsel.

The last thing to go up is the star.

It's best to go to bed early . . .

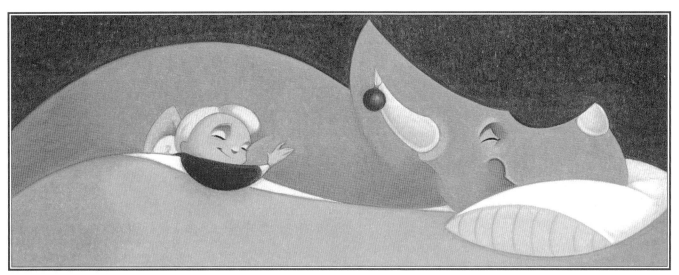

because Santa Claus won't come until you're fast asleep.

And in the morning, just like magic,

Santa Claus has come!

But the real magic of the season is how
Christmas brings everyone together.

FOR SANTA, AND HIS HELPERS.

VIKING

Penguin Young Readers

An Imprint of Penguin Random House LLC

375 Hudson Street

New York, New York 10014

First published in the United States of America by Viking, an imprint of Penguin Random House LLC, 2017

Copyright © 2017 by Molly Idle

LIBRARY OF CONGRESS CATALOGING-IN-PUBLICATION DATA IS AVAILABLE

ISBN 9780425290118

Manufactured in China

3 5 7 9 10 8 6 4 2

Book design by Nancy Brennan   Set in F Caslon Twelve

The illustrations for this book were created with Prismacolor pencils on vellum finish Bristol.